Mattie's Money Tree

Mattie's Money Tree

by Don German
Illustrated by Liisa Chauncy

J
Germ

The Westminster Press
Philadelphia

Book design by Christine Schueler

First edition

Published by The Westminster Press®
Philadelphia, Pennsylvania

PRINTED IN THE UNITED STATES OF AMERICA
2 4 6 8 9 7 5 3 1

Library of Congress Cataloging
in Publication Data

German, Don, 1931–
    Mattie's money tree.

    SUMMARY: Always in need of money, Mattie and
Scott decide to grow it on a grafted tree but when they
set out to spend their first crop they find themselves
giving it away instead.
    1. Children's stories, American. [1. Money—Fiction.
2. Christian life—Fiction] I. Chauncy, Liisa, ill.
II. Title.
PZ7.G297Mat 1984   [Fic]   84-11849
ISBN 0-664-32716-8

*In loving memory
of Cheryl Anne Young*

Contents

I

Mattie's Problem

Mattie had only one problem.

Money.

Not too much money, but too little.

Like a home without a dog or like a super-double cheeseburger without french fries. She didn't even have a supersonic, jet-star, twin-deck stereo cassette player with seventeen push buttons, a carrying handle, and a built-in AM-FM radio, and she wanted one desperately. Even Debbie-the-Dope, Mattie's absolutely worst enemy in the whole world, had a supersonic, jet-star, twin-deck stereo cassette player with seventeen push buttons, a carrying handle, and a built-in AM-FM radio.

Mattie was ten years old, five feet tall, had brown hair, brown eyes, and eight small freckles on her nose, and was called Mattie, which was short for Matilda. She spelled Mattie with an *i-e*.

"That," she said, "is because I'm a girl. Girls' names that rhyme with *e* are spelled with *i-e,* and boys' names that rhyme with *e* are spelled with a *y*. That is, usually they are, but I know a girl named Bobbi and another girl named Toni, and they spell their names with just an *i.* I think that's pretty neat. I wonder if *money* is a boy because it's spelled with a *y?*"

Mattie was out of breath. She was always a little out of breath when she talked, because she had so many important things to say that the words would end up running and tripping over themselves somewhere between her tongue and her teeth.

Her best friend was named Scott, which was his real name and not a nickname at all.

Scott was as shy as Mattie wasn't. His words never left him breathless, because he never used that many. Except when he talked to Mattie. Like Mattie, Scott was ten years old and five feet tall, but he had blond hair and blue eyes, no freckles, and could whistle through his teeth, which Mattie couldn't, no matter how she tried. Maybe some leftover words were caught somewhere in her teeth. Anyway, Scott lived four houses down the street from Mattie. They had been friends for a long, long time, and they shared a lot of friend secrets.

Except for the fact that Scott was a boy and Mattie was a girl, they were the same, only different. For instance, she wore a dress and he wore a suit on special dress-up days, but they both wore blue jeans, T-shirts, and sneakers all the rest of the time.

Scott did not like Debbie either.

"She sure is a dope!" Scott agreed.

But of course she wasn't. Debbie, short for Deborah, was a likable ten-year-old who had one thing for which Mattie and Scott could not forgive her. Lots of money. Debbie's parents not only gave her an allowance of ten dollars a week, they also bought her anything she wanted and a lot she didn't want. Mattie and Scott hated her.

That's the way it goes.

Mattie lived a rather ordinary life in a rather ordinary suburb of Boston. She had nice parents whom she loved and who loved her. She lived in a white frame house that had brown shutters and a copper weathervane horse on the roof. She rode a bike, adored super-double cheeseburgers with french fries, hated brussels sprouts and fishing, and liked Scott, even if he was a boy.

Scott felt the same way about bikes,

Mattie

Scott

Debbie-the-Dope

Fang

Fluffy

dogs, super-double cheeseburgers with french fries, brussels sprouts, and Mattie, even if she was a girl. They were buddies, even if he did like to go fishing and she didn't.

"How would you like to bite into something good, get a sharp hook in your mouth, and then be dragged to shore to get eaten?" she would ask.

Of course, if Scott caught anything, sometimes Mattie would have dinner at his house and help eat it.

Except for that one thing, they agreed on just about everything. Sometimes the other kids would tease, but not too much, because when Scott and Mattie teamed up, they could, if necessary, beat up any other kids in the school. They only had to do it once.

That's the way it goes.

So Mattie had only one big problem. Money.

Mattie's allowance was five dollars a week. So was Scott's. In fact, they pretty much guessed that their parents had an agreement to set their allowances at that amount. Except for Debbie, every kid in the fifth grade got five dollars a week. Suspicious.

"Parents do things like that," Mattie reasoned. "If kids compare notes—and we do—we won't get uptight if we all get the same. At least, that's what parents think."

But if her only big problem was money, just as cats have kittens this brought a bunch of little problems.

"Five dollars a week is a lot of money," said Mattie's dad. "Why, when I was a kid, I only got one dollar a week."

"Yes, but the other day you told me how great it was then," Mattie answered. "Candy bars cost a nickel and movies cost a quarter. Now candy bars cost thirty cents and movies are two dollars."

Five dollars a week was enough for some things, but not enough for a lot of others. It was enough for sixteen and two-thirds candy bars, or two and a half movies, or one super-double cheeseburger and a soda and french fries plus a toy for Mattie's dog, Fang, or for Scott's dog, Fluffy.

"But it isn't enough to buy a brand-new supersonic, jet-star, twin-deck stereo cassette player with seventeen push buttons, a carrying handle, and a built-in AM-FM radio," said Mattie. "And I really want one," she told Scott with a hitch in her voice. "In fact, I don't think I can last much longer without one. Did you see dopey Debbie with hers at the playground the other day?"

"Yeah," Scott said, disgusted. "And five dollars isn't enough to buy matching blue sweatshirts with white letters that say SAVE THE WHALES—DON'T EAT BLUBBER. And Debbie has a red one. that says BAD BREATH IS BETTER THAN NO BREATH AT ALL."

"Yuck! And it isn't enough to buy motors for our bikes," agreed Mattie.

"Or a canoe to put in the Charles River, or a horse for you, or a pet alligator for me," said Scott.

Five dollars was a lot of money in some ways, but in other ways it just wasn't enough. For one thing, it wasn't ten dollars, like Debbie's allowance.

Mattie thought that Mom and Dad earned enough to give her more allowance. Being a whiz-bang wizard at math, she figured it out. Her five dollars a week added up to $260 a year. That sounds like a lot, but it was a little over one half of one percent of what her parents earned. Big deal. A brand-new supersonic, jet-star, twin-deck stereo cassette player with seventeen push buttons, a carrying handle, and a built-in AM-FM radio cost $119.95 at the local discount store.

Of course, Mattie ate her share of the food. She lived comfortably in the warm house. She rode in the family car, and she had nice clothes, even though she always wore blue jeans. And she always got extra money for the things she really needed.

When it came to the things she didn't need but only wanted, her mom said, "Save enough from your allowance."

And if she asked her dad, he said, "Save enough from your allowance."

That's the way it goes.

Mattie did some arithmetic. If she pinched every penny until Lincoln yelled, if she saved all her allowance, which meant no movies, no candy, no ice cream, it would take two years to buy a horse. It would take three years to buy a canoe. And it would take twenty-four weeks just to buy that radio.

From January to June without a single treat? Even a radio with seventeen push buttons wasn't worth that. A person needs a super-double cheeseburger with french fries once in a while!

Mattie tried reasoning with her parents.

"How about a loan?" she asked. "When you buy a car, you borrow the money from the bank. How about if I borrow from you?"

"No way," said Mom. "You can't pay it back. If I loaned you $119.95 for the radio, $500 for the horse, and $800 for the canoe, and you paid me back a dollar a week, it would take over twenty-seven years. You'd be thirty-seven years old. By then, the radio wouldn't work anymore, the horse would have died of old age, the canoe would leak, and you'd be a grown woman arguing with your own kids about their allowances."

"See, that proves I don't get enough allowance," Mattie snapped crossly. "My credit isn't even any good!"

That's the way it goes.

"People don't hire ten-year-old kids," Mattie said to Scott later that day. "We're too young to work at Cheeseburger Corner and too old to sell mud pies."

"We could rob a bank," he suggested.

She punched his arm. "That's dumb!"

"I was only kidding," he said, rubbing his arm. "We could play the stock market and get rich."

"We could also lose everything," Mattie replied. "Besides, I don't think you can play the stock market with ten dollars a week."

They tried their parents again.

"No more money," said Scott's father.

"No more money," said Mattie's mother.

"No more money," said Scott's mother.

"No more money," said Mattie's father. "Do you think money grows on trees?"

And then Mattie had a brilliant idea.

When she and Scott were alone, she whispered, "I have the answer to our

problem. We are going to grow a money tree!"

"Money doesn't grow on trees," said Scott, shaking his head and frowning. "Your dad even said so."

"Right," she said. "It doesn't. But that doesn't mean it can't. Maybe it just means that no one has ever tried it before."

"Aw, you're cuckoo!" he said.

So she punched him in the arm again and walked away.

2

Mattie Finds a Way

Mattie's Girl Scout leader said it was impossible.

Her teacher said it couldn't be done.

Scott's scoutmaster said it was ridiculous.

His uncle, who was a biologist and knew all about trees, said, "Well, if you manage to grow one, be sure to give me some of the seeds."

Mattie told Scott, "If nobody will help us, we'll do it ourselves."

So they decided to figure out a way to

grow a money tree. And they decided to keep it a secret, knowing the grown-ups would forget they had mentioned it. Adults always forget.

Scott thought it was a dumb idea, but if his best friend wanted to try, he would help. Even if it was a waste of time.

That's the way it goes.

Now one thing Mattie knew about trees was that they take a long time to grow. If you take an acorn, which is really a seed for an oak tree, and if you plant that acorn, it will take weeks just to sprout. After it sprouts, it will grow about a foot a year. And the tree won't be big enough to bear its own acorns for about twenty years.

Mattie said, "Look, I can't wait for twenty years. In twenty years, I'll be thirty years old. By then, I won't need money. What would anyone that old spend money on?"

Scott didn't know what to say, so he just looked at her.

"Here, have an apple," he said. "They're from the tree in our backyard."

"That's it!" Mattie shouted. "That's it! If we can't grow a money tree, we'll graft money limbs onto another tree."

"I don't get it," said Scott. "Explain."

"It's simple," she answered eagerly. "I read about it. Apple growers raise some trees that are strong and healthy but maybe don't have such great-tasting apples. Then they cut limbs from trees that do have good-tasting apples and graft them onto the healthy-but-not-so-hot-tasting apple trees. That way, they get good apples and they get them fast! They can even get four or five kinds of apples from the same tree. Now all we need to do is find a healthy tree and graft on some money limbs."

All of that came out in one breath, so her words hit her palate, bounced off the roof of her mouth, slid into her teeth, and tumbled out so fast that she was breathless. But even though some words were jumbled a bit, Scott understood anyway, as friends do.

But he did have some questions.

"What kind of tree?" he asked. "And where do you get money limbs?"

"Wel-l-l-l," gasped Mattie, still out of breath, "I'll have to think about that!"

There was still a little snow on April Fools' Day, when Mattie found the tree she needed. She chose a small paper birch because there was one in the corner of her backyard that no one could see from the road. Also, because it was a paper birch, it was natural that it would grow paper money. And since it was small, she could reach the grafted branches if she stood on a stepladder.

But what kind of limbs could she graft onto it? What would give her a harvest of crisp green bills?

"Aw, give up," said Scott with a sigh. "It can't be done!"

She needed this kind of help from Scott like a picnic needs ants.

Then it happened.

One day near the end of April, Mattie's mother took her to Boston to tour the Federal Reserve Bank. They saw all sorts of interesting things—especially if you think money is interesting. They saw huge machines that sort and count coins. They saw giant computers that whizzed and whirred and clicked and calculated. And they saw a machine that took old, torn, wrinkled bills—one-dollar bills, five-dollar bills, ten-dollar bills, twenty-dollar bills, and even an occasional two-dollar bill—and chopped them into tiny pieces.

Mattie was astonished. "Why are you doing that?" she asked the money chopper. "That's money you're chopping up! Perfectly good money!"

"Because it's worn out." The man laughed. "Going from bank to store to wallet to hand to purse to shop to bank to store wears a dollar bill out in just a year and a half. We used to burn them when they got worn out, but the smoke made people cough. So now we chop up the bills, and then we print brand-new money to take their place."

Mattie's brain waves scampered around inside her head, bouncing from her think tank to her see-screen and back again. She could think even faster than she could talk. And she had an idea. Oh, how she hoped!

"What do you do with that chopped-up money?" she whispered, holding her breath and crossing her fingers.

"We throw it away just to get rid of it. Usually we just send it to the city dump," he said. "Sometimes people like to have it for a souvenir. Some people even spread it on their gardens to keep the weeds from growing."

"May I have some?" asked Mattie in her very best see-how-polite-I-can-be voice. "Just a little?"

"Of course," said the money chopper.

"There's about ten thousand dollars in old bills in that pile. Let me put it in a bag for you."

And he did.

So Mattie left the bank with a big brown paper bag of chopped-up money and plans in the back of her head that kept her brain busy all the way home. Her mom couldn't figure out why she was so quiet. But she knew that when Mattie was quiet, something was about to happen.

3

*Green
Gooey Goop*

Mattie was a mess.

It was after school, while her parents were still at work, and she was standing at the basement laundry tub, smeared with thick, green, gooey goop. Her hair dripped green gooey goop. Her ears were plugged with globs of goop. She was gooey green to the elbows and goopy green to the knees. She was a sticky mess.

She had taken almost all the chopped-up, worn-out ten thousand dollars from the Federal Reserve Bank and carefully mixed them with water and glue to make papier-mâché. If nature hadn't made a tree limb that would grow money, then Mattie would. After all, she had created a ghoul's head for Halloween out of papier-mâché made from shredded-up newspapers. If she could make a ghoul's head, complete with giant, bloody macaroni veins hanging out of the neck, she could make a tree limb.

Or two tree limbs.

Or even three.

And so she did.

First, she took a real tree limb that had blown down in a storm. That was her model. She used an old wire coat hanger as the spine for the limb she was making. She straightened the hanger and then bent it into a curving, irregular shape—just like a tree limb. Then, starting where the limb would join the tree, she began squeezing on the papier-mâché made from the old

money, a bit at a time. Slowly, carefully, she worked, making the limb branch out here, little twigs jut out there. And while she worked, she even got sticky, green, gooey goop in her shoes.

As soon as she finished, she made a second limb and then a third. Then she carefully put the finished work in a warm corner of the basement to dry. After that, she took a bath.

The branches she had made dried nicely. In just a week, Mattie had three lovely limbs, all colored money-green.

She phoned Scott.

"Come on over," she said. "Today is the day we graft the limbs and start our money tree."

Scott thought the idea was silly, but Mattie was his best friend, and friends do silly things for each other. So over to her house he went.

Because Mattie's parents weren't home, the two could work without being seen or interrupted. And did they work! First, they hauled the tall stepladder from the garage.

"Here, let's put it right here," Scott said, "so we can reach that bare spot."

"Good," said Mattie. "Then if any money drops, it will be near the fence and won't blow away. Hand me that brace and bit."

With a carpenter's brace and a one-inch augur bit, Mattie climbed the ladder while Scott steadied it from below. Carefully she made a mark with a pencil.

"There, X marks the spot," she said. "Just like on a treasure map."

And she drilled the first hole, making it deep enough to hold the limb, then daubing it with glue.

"Hand me the first limb," she instructed, and Scott did.

The limb slid into the hole as if made for it—as, indeed, it was.

Then Scott took a turn and grafted on the second limb, and then Mattie did the third. Finally, after they put away

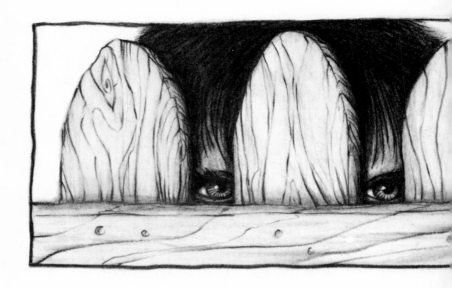

the stepladder and the brace and bit,
Mattie sprinkled the last unused bits of
chopped money around the base of the
tree. "Fertilizer," she said. "Now we
just wait for the harvest."

Mattie's parents' car pulled into the
driveway as she and Scott, who was
whistling through his teeth as though
he hadn't a care in the world, came
around to the front of the house.

"Hi, Mom and Dad!" said Mattie.

"Hi, kids. What have you been up to
this afternoon?" asked her father.

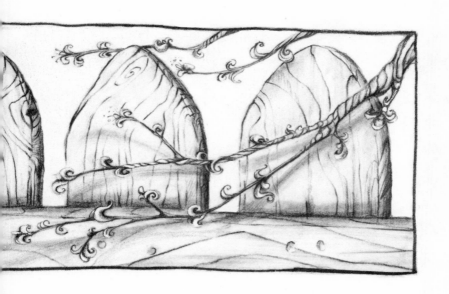

"Oh," Mattie said, knowing that her parents weren't paying any attention, "we're just growing a money tree."

"That's nice, dear," said her mother.

What Mattie and Scott didn't know was that, just beyond the fence, someone had been watching their every move. Now that someone smiled and walked slowly up the street.

4

Success!

Mattie's and Scott's allowances of five dollars a week came and went, again and again. April rained into May, the lilacs budded, the maples budded, and—miracle!

"Scott, get over here!" Mattie phoned excitedly. "Our money limbs have buds on them! Hundreds of buds! Thousands of buds! We're going to be rich!"

Now Scott had never really believed that Mattie's scheme would work, but if Mattie said buds, that meant buds. She might be a little crazy, but she wasn't dumb. He put down the phone and was in Mattie's backyard in one minute and seven seconds flat. Mattie was waiting.

"First," he said, panting and out of breath, "we get a supersonic, jet-star, twin-deck stereo cassette player with seventeen push buttons, a carrying handle, and a built-in AM-FM radio."

"No," Mattie said, "we get two of them! One for each of us! Then, when we go to the beach, we can each listen to whatever we want."

"But we always want to listen to the same thing anyway," said Scott.

"Never mind, we're rich!" Mattie said with a grin.

"Okay," agreed Scott. "Then we'll get canoes and horses and pet alligators and sweatshirts that say SAVE THE WHALES—DON'T EAT BLUBBER."

"Let's sit under our money tree and watch it grow," said Mattie.

And they tried. But trees, even money trees, grow so slowly that Mat-

tie and Scott couldn't see a thing.
That's the way it goes.

Things you can't see happen in a minute do happen in days, and the limbs grew and the buds multiplied and began to open. In a week, the three grafted limbs were covered with thousands and thousands of budding one-dollar bills, five-dollar bills, ten-dollar bills, twenty-dollar bills, and even a few two-dollar bills. Mattie was tickled pink because she was a girl. Scott was tickled pink too, even though he was a boy, because no one can be tickled blue.

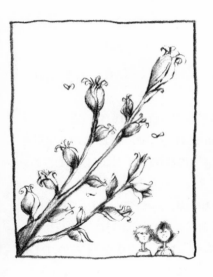 

May flowers had bloomed into lush, warm days when, on the tenth of June, two wonderful things happened. First, Scott and Mattie finished the school year and, naturally, got promoted.

But the second thing was even better. They picked their first small crop of money—six one-dollar bills, three five-dollar bills, and one ten-dollar bill.

Now Mattie and Scott hadn't exactly been keeping their money tree a secret, they just hadn't told anyone about it. After all, burglars could come in the night and pick all the money. And their parents hadn't believed in the idea anyway, so . . . well, they just didn't tell, that's all.

They took their small but profitable first crop to Scott's house. His parents were out, and they could make plans in peace.

"Well," Mattie said, sprawling on the living room couch, "we could split it and have fifteen dollars and fifty cents each. Or we could save it toward our first supersonic, jet-star, twin-deck stereo cassette player with seventeen push buttons, a carrying handle, and a built-in AM-FM radio. Or—"

Scott interrupted. "We could invest in the stock market. Or buy some gold. I heard my dad say that gold could make you rich. Or—"

"You've got a thought there, Scott," said Mattie, not letting him finish. "Let's put it in the bank and start to save for our first supersonic, jet-star, twin-deck stereo cassette player with seventeen push buttons, a carrying handle, and a built-in AM-FM radio."

And they did.

Or at least they tried.

As they were walking to the bank, they passed a bag lady sitting propped against a wall, surrounded by two worn shopping bags, a soiled, torn quilt, and a bundle of ragged clothes. Even towns as prosperous as theirs had an occasional poor unfortunate person who lived on the streets. Surprised to see her, they felt a little guilty as they passed.

The bag lady looked awfully hungry. And they had gone without a supersonic, jet-star, twin-deck stereo cassette player with seventeen push buttons, a carrying handle, and a built-in AM-FM radio for a long time so . . .

"I have an idea," said Scott, who had a lump in his throat.

"I do too," said Mattie. "Let's do it."

So they did.

They had felt funny picking money from their money tree. Like they had maybe been doing something wrong.

But now they had done something they knew was right. They felt good about it, and so did the bag lady, who was thirty-one dollars richer.

"Wait!" said the bag lady as they started to walk away. "Wait a minute. Did you know that I can tell fortunes? Here, show me your hands and let me tell yours."

She took their small clean hands in her grimy, calloused ones and peered closely at them.

"You are very nice," she said thoughtfully, "but I knew that before I saw your hands. And you're going to have some strange experiences—soon! I see here that four things are going to happen to you. You're going to:

"Cheat a friend,
Meet a friend,
Miss a friend,
Kiss a friend.

"And at the same time you're going to grow up. And it's going to hurt a little."

"What does that mean?" asked Scott.

"You'll have to wait to find out," said the bag lady. "I tell you only what I see."

5

A Prediction Comes True

The next morning Scott woke up extra early and ran to Mattie's backyard. He got there first. Mattie was nowhere in sight, but on the tree a new crop of bills rustled in the morning breeze.

Right in front of Scott's nose a crisp new twenty-dollar bill waved to him.

Pick me, the bill seemed to say. *Pick me and I'll buy you a siren for your bike. Better yet, I'll buy that fishing rod you've been wanting.*

Mattie didn't like fishing, so, Scott thought, she would never go along with that.

Now the bill was singing to him.

Pick me, pick me, pick me, pick-mepickmepickme—I'm YOURS!

Scott picked the twenty-dollar bill and quickly stuffed it in his pocket.

He looked over his left shoulder.

He looked over his right shoulder.

"Hi, Scott!" called Mattie, coming out of her back door. "How's our crop look?"

"Shhh," shushed Scott nervously. "Where are your folks?"

"At work, naturally," said Mattie. "Where do you think they would be on a Tuesday morning? Oh, look!" she exclaimed. "Here's a five, and a ten, and another five, and two ones—look, here's even a two-dollar bill! Oh, Scott, hold out your hands while I pick!"

Seventy-four dollars later, Mattie finished picking.

"Tomorrow, we'll have $119.95 plus

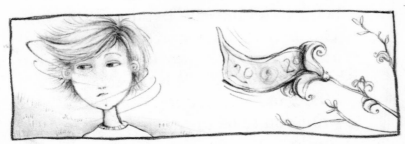

tax, and we can buy a supersonic, jet-star, twin-deck stereo cassette player with seventeen push buttons, a carrying handle, and a built-in AM-FM radio —for you!" she said triumphantly.

"For me?" asked Scott. He felt awful about snitching the twenty-dollar bill. "The money tree was your idea, and you did most of the work. The first radio should be for you. Why me?"

"Because you are my best friend and I want you to be first," said Mattie with a smile.

The twenty-dollar bill in Scott's pocket seemed to grow heavier and heavier.

"Look," he said, poking the ground with the toe of his sneaker, "this is dumb. You grew the tree, so you get first chance to spend the money. Go buy a dress or something."

"When did you ever see me wear a dress except for Easter?" Mattie laughed. "Or want a dress? What I do want is to do something nice for you. I have it! Let's take twenty dollars and go downtown and buy that fishing rod you've been wanting for the Trout Derby! We can get the stereo the day after tomorrow."

"But you don't like fishing," argued Scott, who by now was really hurting inside.

"What has that got to do with anything?" said Mattie. "The fishing rod is for you, not me. You're the one who will murder the fish, not me. But I will help eat them! Come on, let's go."

And she dragged Scott down the street. By now, the hidden twenty-dollar bill was so heavy that Scott wanted to cry—and he hadn't cried in a long time.

But he went, and he didn't cry.

Reluctantly, Scott followed Mattie into the sporting goods store. The clerk smiled.

"Hi, kids," he said. "Looking at bike motors again?"

"Nope," said Mattie, "fishing rods.

Specifically, we're looking for a five-foot fiberglass fly rod with a magnesium reel seat that Scott can use on the Sudbury River—which is silly to call a river since it's only ten feet wide and not deep enough to get your knees wet, and I think fishing is dumb anyway, but it's for Scott, so that's okay."

That was a tongue-tripping Mattie-mouthful.

But the clerk said, "Gee, I'm sorry, but I just sold my last fiberglass stream rod. Next Saturday's the Trout Derby, you know, so a lot of folks want one. But I'll have more in a few days."

Mattie's face fell. Scott's didn't. He had a temporary reprieve.

As they left the shop and walked down the busy sidewalk, they passed an old man selling pencils. Like the bag lady, he too was new in town. And he was pitiable. Both legs were gone, he was dressed in tattered clothes, and he hadn't shaved in a week. His empty pants legs were folded under him, and he sat on a little platform on wheels. He held a box filled with cheap wooden pencils.

Scott spied him first.

"Look, Mattie," he said, "we've got to help him."

"Fine," she answered, "but I'm keeping enough money to buy your fly rod."

"No," said Scott. "I've decided to give up fishing anyway."

So the beggar, used to getting a nickel here and a dime there, was suddenly presented with seventy-four dollars in crisp new bills. He smiled a crooked smile at the two young people.

"God bless," he said softly, a tear rolling down one grimy cheek.

Upset at seeing the man's misery, Mattie and Scott started to walk quickly away.

"Wait!" the man called to them.

They stopped and turned.

"The first prediction has come true," the beggar went on. "One down and three to go."

He turned away, and, moving his platform with two leather mitts, he quickly rolled around the corner.

"Wait!" cried Mattie. "Please! Wait!"

But by the time she and Scott reached the corner, the beggar had disappeared.

"What did he mean?" said Mattie. "Which prediction? How does he know about the bag lady?"

Cheat a friend,
Meet a friend,
Miss a friend,
Kiss a friend flashed through her mind. Then she drew in her breath. "Did he mean that my promising you a fishing rod and then giving him the money was cheating you? Oh, Scott, I'm so sorry!"

"Nuts," Scott said, concentrating very hard on kicking a pebble. "You didn't cheat me. He's just a poor sick old man. Forget it."

But Mattie didn't forget, and neither did Scott.

6

Debbie-the-Dope

Scott had disappeared!

It had been the last day of June when Scott picked the twenty-dollar bill and didn't tell Mattie. Now the first day of July was warm and sunny, and, as usual, Mattie ran to her backyard to meet him.

No Scott.

She ran to his backyard.

Still no Scott.

She rang his doorbell. Scott's mother answered the door.

"Hi, Mrs. Madigan," said Mattie. "Is Scott around?"

"You mean he's not with you?" exclaimed Scott's mother. "But he's always with you. I haven't seen him this morning . . . that's strange! Not like Scott at all."

"Thanks anyway, Mrs. Madigan," said Mattie. "I guess he just had an errand or something. I'll see him later."

"Hmmm," hmmed Mrs. Madigan. "Strange! Well, bye, Mattie. I'm sure he'll be back soon. When he comes in, I'll tell him to call you."

But the hours passed and no call came.

Where in the world was Scott? Every day for the past year, except when his Scout troop went on camporee and when she had had her tonsils out, he and Mattie had gotten together first thing every morning.

Today he was nowhere to be seen.

Now Mattie without Scott was like vanilla without chocolate, peanut butter without jelly, or a super-double cheeseburger without cheese. She hadn't had time to get really lonely, but she did miss him.

And she did have her money tree to tend.

On Monday, she picked $82, then went skating in the park. Alone.

On Tuesday, she picked $57, then rode her bike the whole afternoon. Alone.

On Wednesday, she picked $24, then sat in her yard and read a book, which was nice, but it wasn't Scott. Alone.

On Thursday, she picked a record crop of $128 and rang Scott's bell again. She didn't like to ring his bell and ask for him. It was kind of embarrassing, even if they were best friends, and even if his folks were very nice.

"Hi, Mrs. Madigan," she said. "Where's Scott?"

"I can't imagine," said his mother. "Every morning he leaves here about seven o'clock. When I ask him where

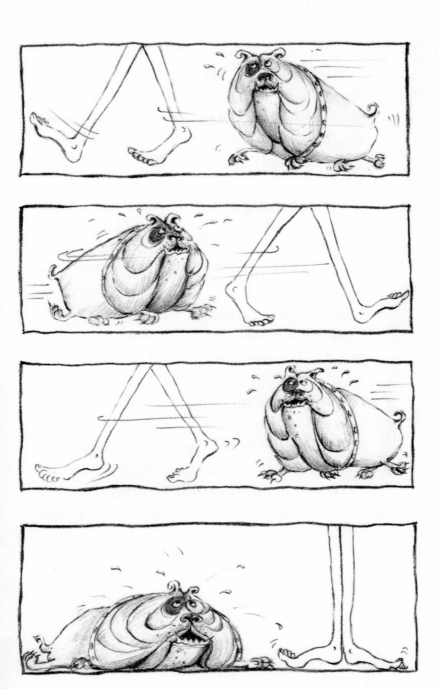

he's going, he always says, 'There's something I've got to do for Mattie—and it's okay, Mom, but it's a secret.' And then he leaves. He's a good boy, so I don't push him, but I am getting a little concerned."

"Something for me?" Mattie was puzzled. "He doesn't have to do anything for me—or at least, nothing that I know of."

Strange.

By Friday, Mattie was really upset. The money crop that day was small—only $24—so she picked it and then went to the playground, alone. And then, to top off a really rotten week, there was just one other person in the park. Debbie-the-Dope. With her supersonic, jet-star, twin-deck stereo cassette player with seventeen push buttons, a carrying handle, and a built-in AM-FM radio!

Mattie tried to escape without being seen.

No such luck.

"Hi, Mattie!" Debbie-the-Dope called. "I'm over here."

"Whoop-de-do," muttered Mattie. "Who cares?"

Out loud she said, "Oh, hi, Debbie," and walked toward her.

"Where's Scott?" asked Debbie.

"Why, he's—he's—he's doing something important, for me," said Mattie.

"What?" asked Debbie.

"Well, it's a secret," Mattie said.

"But I won't tell," said Debbie. "So tell me."

Mattie was embarrassed.

"The truth is," said Mattie, "I don't know what the secret is."

"Well," said Debbie, "I guess it wouldn't be a secret if you knew what it was. Maybe he has a new friend. Hey, maybe you and I can spend the day together. I'd like that."

Inwardly, Mattie groaned.

But she was polite and said, "That would be okay."

Mattie thought to herself that a day

with Debbie might be almost as much fun as a grammar test, or even a trip to the dentist or getting run over by a bus. She wanted to be with Scott. But she spent the day with Debbie.

That's the way it goes.

It was funny, but she hadn't spent a penny of the money-tree money. Just having it made Mattie need to spend less. She didn't have to buy this candy bar or that book. So she had saved two whole weeks' allowance, and she had it with her.

First, Mattie and Debbie went to the variety store on Main Street and bought lipstick, and Debbie showed Mattie how to put it on. Mattie would never have worn lipstick with Scott around.

Then they went to Cheeseburger Corner for super-double cheeseburgers with french fries and root beer.

Finally, they went to the movies and saw a movie that Scott hadn't wanted

to see and ate big boxes of popcorn with double butter.

As the day was ending, Mattie realized that she had had a lot of fun. Debbie hadn't played her supersonic, jet-star, twin-deck stereo cassette player with seventeen push buttons, a carrying handle, and a built-in AM-FM radio all day.

"Why don't you play your stereo?" asked Mattie.

"Oh," said Debbie, "I don't even like the dumb thing. I only play it when I haven't got a friend like you to be with. My dad gave me the stereo. I didn't really want it, but I carry it around so he'll think I like it and so I won't hurt his feelings. I think sometimes my folks give me things to keep me out of their hair."

Somehow Debbie's stereo didn't seem so shiny and attractive and desirable anymore.

Mattie didn't ask Debbie how it felt to be rich, because now she was richer than Debbie. Of course, she didn't tell Debbie about the money or the money tree. And she hadn't spent any of the bills she had picked, because she was saving them to split with her partner, Scott. But just knowing the money was there gave her a rich feeling, and she didn't have to be—what? Jealous? Mattie, jealous of Debbie?

Yes, she admitted it. Just having all that money under her spare blue jeans in the second bureau drawer made her feel rich, and she didn't have to be jealous anymore.

And when she wasn't being jealous of Debbie, she discovered something. At the variety store, she had had fun. At Cheeseburger Corner, she had had fun. At the movies, she had had fun. She had discovered that Debbie wasn't a dope after all. Debbie had a little too much money maybe, but Mattie also had money these days. And Debbie was nice enough so that Mattie ended the day with a question.

"What are you doing tomorrow?" she wanted to know.

"Let's go swimming," answered Debbie, pleased as punch to have finally found a friend.

And they agreed to do just that.

On the way home, Mattie passed a pretty little girl strapped into leg braces and using crutches. The girl was nicely dressed, but she looked sad as she slowly made her way down the sidewalk. Mattie felt very sorry that the little girl couldn't run and jump and

ride a bike. She didn't like to look at
her, but she couldn't stop. She wished
she had some of the money-tree money
with her to give to the girl, but she
didn't. And the girl didn't seem to be
poor, just disabled, so Mattie forced
herself to smile and say hello.

The little girl smiled back and softly
said something. Mattie had to strain to
catch her words.

She spoke again, in a shy little-girl
voice.

"Hello, Mattie," she said. "That's two
down and two to go."

Mattie's jaw dropped, and she stood frozen as the girl smiled and hobbled away.

Mattie was so shocked she ran all the way home. In fact, she was so shocked that she never even saw Scott hiding in the bushes, listening to her and the pretty little girl.

7

Scott's Secret

Where had Scott been?

July was ending, and Mattie hadn't spent any time with him for a whole month. She hadn't spent so many days without Scott in years. Naturally she was upset, but how could she know that Scott was avoiding her because he felt so awful about picking the twenty-dollar bill when she wasn't looking?

She and Debbie had seen a lot of movies and done a lot of shopping, much of it for girl stuff that she never would have bought if she had been with Scott.

She bought another lipstick.

She bought a box of seven panties, each a different color, each embroidered with the name of a different day of the week.

She bought a small bottle of toilet water.

And, to cap it off, she even bought a training bra, though she didn't need one yet.

Debbie was fun, but Mattie missed Scott.

Terribly.

Twice she had seen him. Once he was a block away, and she called and called to him as she ran to catch up, but he was running too fast and soon left her behind.

The other time, she got up early and waited by his door. As he came out, she grabbed his arm.

"Scott, what's wrong?" she said. "Where have you been? What did I do? Why aren't we friends anymore?"

Scott turned red with embarrassment.

"Look, Mattie," he said, "I miss you too. And I am your friend, and I'll be back. But I have something I have to do, and it's a secret that I can't tell you now, but I will soon. Till then, you'll just have to trust me. Not that you should."

He hung his head, and then he ran away.

Strange.

Mattie didn't try to follow Scott. Her feelings were too hurt. And if he said it was okay, it was okay. But she was very lonely, and she wondered what was going on.

And all this time, Mattie was picking money. July had been a perfect month for growing anything—lots of sun and just enough rain to make Mattie's mom's roses grow and tumble, all red and white and yellow, down the back fence. And the corn that Mattie's dad raised grew tall and extra sweet. The lettuce grew leafy enough to tempt any rabbit, and the tomatoes decorated the bushy vines like tasty Christmas-tree decorations.

Every day, as soon as her folks left for work, Mattie dashed to the backyard and picked money. She didn't think there was anything wrong with her growing one- and five- and ten- and twenty-dollar bills, with an occasional two-dollar bill scattered in. But for some reason she never told her parents, and she carefully picked each day's crop before they could come home from work and see the money dangling from the limbs she had grafted onto the tree.

By the middle of July, she had collected over $1,000. By the end of July, she had over $5,000 in the bureau drawer under her spare blue jeans. And she hadn't spent one cent of it. She was still waiting to share it with Scott.

The question was, Where was Scott?

And the answer was that he was on the other side of town busily pushing a lawn mower back and forth, back and forth, neatly trimming the grass in front of a house that Mattie had never seen. And when he finished mowing, he would go to another house to pull weeds and to another one to cut the grass.

The answer was that Scott was working and working hard. And he didn't have $5,000 as Mattie did, but he did have over $100, and he had earned it all by himself.

One day, as Mattie came home after a day of swimming with Debbie, she passed a kitten that had been hurt in an accident. The gray and white animal limped to Mattie and held out its wounded paw for help. Mattie picked it up and cuddled it.

"Poor kitty," she said. "I'll get you fixed up. I'll take you to our vet and let him bandage that paw."

And as she walked down the street

toward the animal clinic, the kitten purred and snuggled close. She wished that Scott were there to help care for the kitten. She missed him more every day. But now she had to do something for the little cat.

"I'm going to get you fixed up and give you to Debbie," Mattie said. "She needs a pet and you need a home."

The kitten, eyes closed, purred contentedly.

And Mattie could have sworn that the purring said, "That's three, Mattie. One to go."

8

Partners Again

It was August first, and it was a beautiful New England day. Today it would be about eighty degrees—just perfect swimming weather—and tonight it would be cool enough for Mattie to shiver a little, if she still had on her shorts, and to sleep comfortably under just one thin blanket.

As usual, after her parents left for work, Mattie went to the garden to pick the money. This day, she could see that she had a big harvest waiting. But it was no fun picking it without someone to share it.

She had just reached for a ten-dollar bill when from behind a tree—

"Hi, Mattie, need some help?"

Mattie jumped.

It was Scott!

"Scott," she cried. "Where have you been? What have you been doing? Who have you been with? Why haven't you come to be with me? Are you mad at me? What did I do? Should I be mad at you? I've been seeing Debbie, and she's not a dope at all and—oh, Scott!"

And the words were coming out so fast that they hit Mattie's front teeth, bounced back in her throat, and got so twisted up that all the boy understood was, "Oh, Scott."

"Here," Scott said. "This is for you."

And he took a large, beautifully wrapped package out from behind a tree.

"For me?" Mattie said. "Why for me?"

"Open it," said Scott.

And Mattie did.

And Mattie gasped.

For inside was a brand-new supersonic, jet-star, twin-deck stereo cassette player with seventeen push buttons, a carrying handle, and a built-in AM-FM radio.

And taped to the supersonic, jet-star, twin-deck stereo cassette player with seventeen push buttons, a carrying handle, and a built-in AM-FM radio was a twenty-dollar bill.

For once in her life, Mattie was speechless.

"What—why—" she croaked.

"When you weren't here," confessed Scott, "I picked a twenty-dollar bill. I was going to keep it, to buy a fishing rod. And I felt so guilty, I couldn't face you. Then you wanted to buy me a rod from the money you grew. You were so nice, and I was rotten. So I spent the whole month working on people's gardens and lawns, and I saved the money and bought you the cassette player you wanted. And here's the twenty dollars I took."

It was the longest speech Scott had ever made.

Mattie was still speechless.

If Mattie had not been a person who didn't cry, Scott might have noticed something shiny in the corners of her brown eyes.

"You didn't steal anything," she said.

"Yes, I did," Scott said.

"No," Mattie insisted. "You can only steal when you take what doesn't belong to you. That money is as much yours as mine. You can't steal from yourself."

Scott shook his head. He had a couple of shiny spots in his eyes too.

"No," Scott said, "that's nice of you to say, but I meant to take the money and not tell you and not share it with you."

Mattie thought about this.

"Okay," she said. "So you think you

meant to take it and not tell me. But you didn't. You put it back. And we're friends, and I don't care anyway. Except for one thing."

"What's that?" asked Scott.

"Don't ever stay away again without telling me why and where you're going," Mattie replied. "I missed you. A lot."

Then Mattie looked at Scott.

"I have something to confess too," she said. "While you were gone, I saw a lot of Debbie. And like I said, she's not a dope at all, just lonely."

Mattie spoke slowly, her words not jumbled at all.

"And I learned something," she said. "I learned that I was the dope, not her. She didn't have a friend, but I have you. I have nice parents, but hers give her things and money and don't pay any attention to her. I'm happy and she's not. And yet I was dumb enough to be jealous of her."

Mattie went on. "And, Scott," she

said, "I'm so pleased that you worked so hard for me, but I have to tell you that I don't want a supersonic, jet-star, twin-deck stereo cassette player with seventeen push buttons, a carrying handle, and a built-in AM-FM radio. I want you back. And I want us to be friends with Debbie. And I don't even care too much about more allowance."

And not one word had got stuck on the roof of her mouth.

That's the way it goes.

Mattie and Scott worked together picking the money crop. Then they went to Mattie's room, where she got the stack of bills from under her extra blue jeans.

They counted.

"Eight thousand dollars . . ."

"Nine thousand and ten dollars . . ."

"Nine thousand six hundred and sixty-three dollars . . ."

"Nine thousand eight hundred and seventy-five dollars . . ."

"Oh," said Scott, "don't forget the twenty dollars I gave back. Here it is."

Mattie added it to the stack.

"Nine thousand eight hundred and ninety-five dollars!" she cried. "Oh, Scott, we're rich, really rich!"

And at that the doorbell rang.

Mattie and Scott quickly stuffed the money into a big brown paper bag. Then they ran down the stairs and opened the front door. A nicely dressed woman in a business suit stood there smiling at them.

"Hello," she said. "Are you Mattie? And Scott?"

"Yes, we are," said Mattie.

"I'm Susan Swann," the woman said, stepping inside. "I've come for the money. It was so nice of you to grow it for us. The disabled children and the sick old people and the animals will appreciate it so much."

"The money?" Mattie asked. "The children? The sick old people? The animals? What money? What children?

What sick old people? What animals?"

Mattie's heart was in her throat as she waited for the answers.

Susan Swann smiled. "Why, the disabled children at the summer camp. The sick old people at the nursing home. The animals at the shelter. You know, the people and animals that you and Scott have been growing the money for."

"But we've been growing it to buy supersonic, jet-star, twin-deck stereo cassette players with seventeen push buttons, carrying handles, and built-in AM-FM radios," said Mattie, her voice cracking just a bit.

"I don't ever want to see another supersonic, jet-star, twin-deck stereo cassette player with seventeen push buttons, a carrying handle, and a built-in AM-FM radio," said Scott.

"And we were going to buy canoes and horses and motorbikes and fancy sweatshirts that say SAVE THE WHALES —DON'T EAT BLUBBER," Mattie said.

"I don't want them either," Scott said. "Well, maybe I would like the sweatshirt."

"Miss Swann," Mattie asked, "how did you know about the money?"

"Because I chose you to grow it for us," Susan Swann replied. "And you did a good job, too. The best ever."

"You mean other people have grown money trees?" Scott asked.

"Oh, a few," said Susan Swann, "a few. And some are growing them now, and more will next year and the next. Every now and then we come across someone who is smart enough and nice enough to do it for us, and this time we were lucky enough to find *two* nice people—you and Scott."

"But I'm not nice," said Scott. "You don't know me very well."

"Nonsense," said Susan Swann. "You don't know yourself very well. You *are* nice. And now, the ten thousand dollars, please."

"Who are you?" asked Mattie. "Why should we give you the money?"

"I told you who I am. I'm Susan Swann," the woman said. "And you'll give me the money because you want to. You see, you have all the things money can't buy—health, happiness, friends—but some people need money to try to buy at least a part of those things. You gave the bag lady money for food and a place to sleep. You gave the man with no legs money for the same things. You gave the disabled girl a warm smile and a hello, and that was better than money because not many people are friendly to her. You gave the kitten back its health. And now you're going to give lots more."

"Yes," said Mattie. "I guess we are."

And she ran up and got the bag of money. But she held on to it.

"First," said Mattie, hesitating, "tell me one thing. Who are you really? And how do you know us? And how do you know about the bag lady and the beggar and the little girl and the kitten? And, Miss Swann, we don't have ten thousand dollars—not quite."

Susan Swann smiled as she reached for the bag.

"That's right," she said. "You already gave me some of it. Today I may be Susan Swann, but in your past I was a bag lady and a beggar and a disabled child and a hurt kitten. Tomorrow, I shall be—well, if you meet me, you'll know."

She took the money, leaned over and kissed first Mattie and then Scott, then turned to leave.

"Still one prediction to go," she said, closing the door.

Mattie looked at Scott.

"What does that mean?" he asked.

"This," said Mattie, throwing her arms around Scott's neck and giving him a kiss. "Welcome back, friend."

And with that they ran to their money tree. But when they got there, the limbs they had so carefully grafted

on were gone. All that was left were three rusty, straightened coat hangers sticking out of the trunk.

"Well," said Mattie, "do you think anyone will ever believe us?"

"Only someone else she chose to grow a money tree," replied Scott.

"You're right," said Mattie, "so we won't tell a soul. Now let's take that brand-new supersonic, jet-star, twin-deck stereo cassette player with seventeen push buttons, a carrying handle, and a built-in AM-FM radio to the store where you bought it and get the money back. Then let's buy three sweatshirts that say SAVE THE WHALES—DON'T EAT BLUBBER and put the rest in the bank. And I'll help you cut some more grass, and we can really save some money."

"Great," said Scott. "But why three sweatshirts?"

"Well," said Mattie, grinning, "one for Debbie, naturally."

It seems that Mattie and Scott were growing up.

That's the way it goes.

About the Author

DON GERMAN has been a full-time professional writer since 1964 and is the author or co-author of 23 books. With his wife, Joan, and a West Highland white terrier named Robbie, he lives two miles up the side of West Mountain in Cheshire, Massachusetts. Mr. German likes organic gardening and does all the family cooking. He has appeared on television and radio and enjoys it when people think he is funny.

J
GERM   10.95
GERMAN   WESTMINSTER
MATTIE'S MONEY TREE

DATE DUE		
AUG 0 2 2006